Genevieve has a very-very Periwinkle Day

Story by Karlene Kay Ryan • Pictures by Meredith Johnson

"If you truly love nature, you will find beauty everywhere."
~Vincent Van Gogh

This Genevieve story represents Karlene Kay Ryan's prayer for hope and healing for all children diagnosed with cancer.

Karlene Kay Ryan supports The Periwinkle Foundation, www.periwinklefoundation.org

The Periwinkle Foundation develops and provides programs that positively change the lives of children, young adults, and families who are challenged by cancer.

The Foundation's "Making a Mark Program" is an exhibition of art and creative writing by children touched by cancer and blood disorders. Texas Children's Cancer Center, Making a Mark Program: www.txch.org/arts-in-medicine/making-a-mark/

The color periwinkle may represent serenity, calmness, or stomach cancer awareness. Alkaloids from Vinca plants (common name: periwinkle) are used as chemotherapy agents.

Wipe Out Kids' Cancer: www.wokc.org

Valley Children's Healtcare and The Craycroft Cancer Center: www.valleychildrens.org/Services/medical/oncology

My heartfelt gratitude to Ann Remen-Willis, Siri Weber Feeney,
Meredith Johnson, who inspired and launched my world as an author of children's books.
~Karlene Kay Ryan

Printed in the United States by Bookmasters, Inc., 30 Amberwood Parkway, Ashland, OH 44805
September 2016, Job #50015514

Summary: When Genevieve misses a long-looked-forward-to beach outing with her class, she finds out Periwinkle is not only her favorite color, but it can be a healing one, too!

Library of Congress Control Number: 2015919552
ISBN-13:   978-0-9888843-8-0

KKR

Karlene Kay Ryan
www.karlenekayryan.com

To
Mayo Ryan, Sr.
who loves
his children
and his
grandchildren

The sun was up and so was Genevieve.

At the playground, Genevieve ran over to her friends.

Miss Janice rang the bell.

Good morning, children.
Come inside.
We have lots to do
to get ready for our
trip tomorrow!

"I love the beach," said Miss Janice.
"I love the sound of the waves and the
seagulls. Alisha, Sam, what do
you like about the beach?"

The water!

Sandcastles!

What's Periwinkle?

It's my very-very favorite color! Like my t-shirt!

That looks purple.

It's not purple and it's not lavender. It's special!

Periwinkle ocean! Periwinkle sky! Periwinkle makes me happy — and tomorrow's going to be a very-very periwinkle day!

Genevieve woke up early the next day.

She put on her
periwinkle sundress
and . . .

her brand-new periwinkle
flip-flops and . . .

picked up her pretty
periwinkle towel.

But somehow, they just didn't make her smile.

Last of all, Genevieve brushed her hair and put on her sparkle-y periwinkle sunglasses.

She looked very periwinkle-y, but it didn't make her smile.

She was trying to feel happy. She tried to think about all the things she and her friends would do at the beach, when . . .

Mommy and Daddy helped Genevieve and took her temperature.

At school, Miss Janice started the day.

Good morning,
children.
I'm sad to say that
Genevieve is sick
and won't
be able to come with
us today!

It was a beautiful day.

The sky is periwinkle.

The water is a little bit periwinkle, too.
It shines like a periwinkle rainbow!

On the way back to school, Sam, Alisha,
Maria and Timothy talked to Miss Janice.

They worked hard
the rest of the afternoon . . ..